# Adelaide and the Night Train

# Adelaide and the Night Train

by Liz Rosenberg    Paintings by Lisa Desimini

A Charlotte Zolotow Book

Harper & Row, Publishers

Library of Congress Cataloging-in-Publication Data
Rosenberg, Liz.
    Adelaide and the night train / by Liz Rosenberg ; paintings by
Lisa Desimini.
        p.      cm.
    "A Charlotte Zolotow Book."
    Summary: Before falling asleep, a little girl takes a ride on a
train and watches through a window as the nighttime world goes by.
    ISBN 0-06-025102-6 : $        .  ISBN 0-06-025103-4 (lib. bdg.) :
$
    [1. Railroads—Trains—Fiction.   2. Bedtime—Fiction.   3. Sleep—
Fiction.   4. Night—Fiction.]   I. Desimini, Lisa, ill.   II. Title.
PZ7.R71894Ad  1989                                      88-39948
[E]—dc 19                                                   CIP
                                                            AC

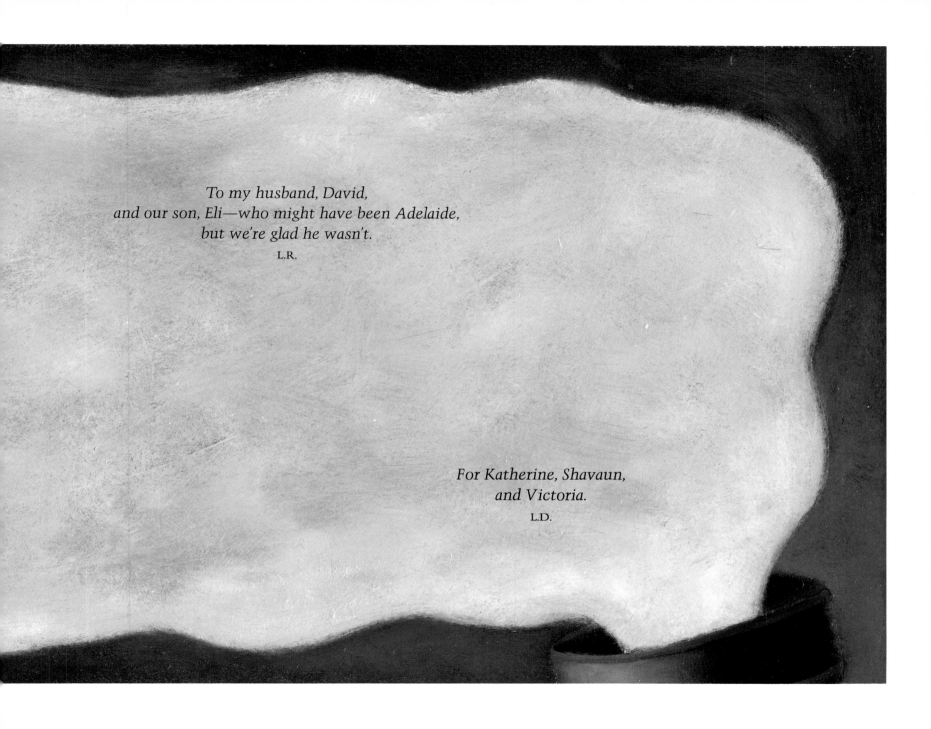

*To my husband, David,*
*and our son, Eli—who might have been Adelaide,*
*but we're glad he wasn't.*

L.R.

*For Katherine, Shavaun,*
*and Victoria.*

L.D.

One warm, spring night, Adelaide could not fall asleep. All her brothers and sisters were in bed. Her mother and father were asleep. Even her dog was curled up at her feet, dreaming of chasing rabbits.

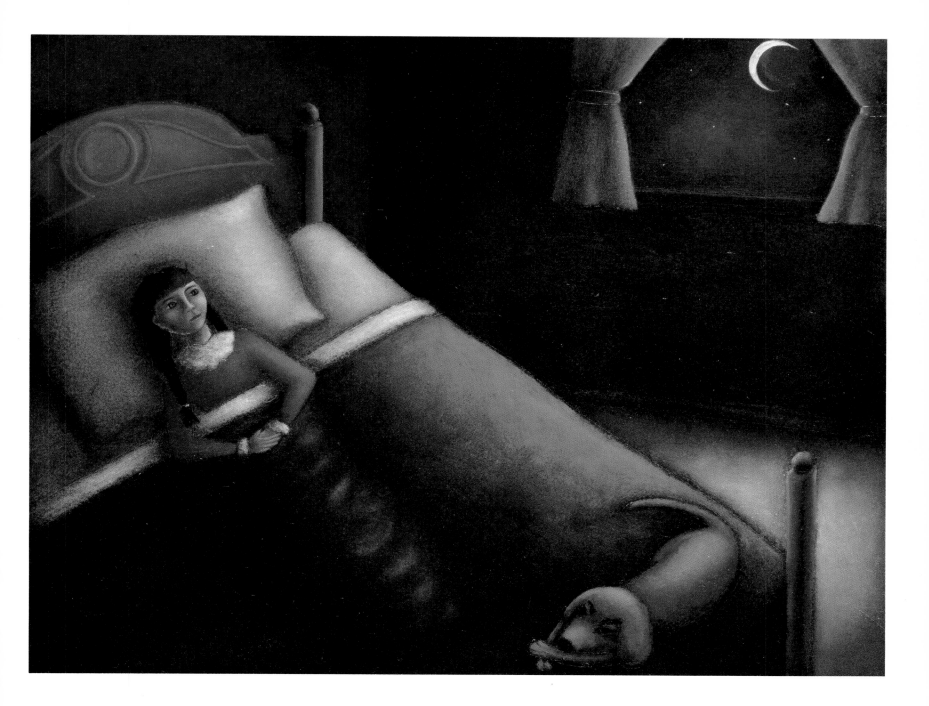

The hall light was out, and the streets were dark and silent. Now and then a train passed by behind the house. The railroad crossing bells would ring softly. Lights from the train window fluttered on the grass. The train horn would grow loud, and then softer. Adelaide loved it when the train passed by. But afterward the night seemed even darker and quieter than before. Only Adelaide was awake. "I have lost my way to sleep," she said. Then…

"All aboard!" cried the conductor. He put out his hand and helped Adelaide up the metal steps. And the train set off into the night.

They passed a field where rabbits sat on their hind legs and watched the train go by. They passed a slow-moving river. An owl glided beside the train as noiselessly as a falling leaf.

They passed the restless ocean, combing out her hair. The hem of her long gown dragged like lace on the shore. The lighthouse blinked sleepily but stayed awake.

Four firemen played cards.

A night watchman sat in his car and read by flashlight.

Two girls stayed up all night and talked.

Frogs practiced their singing.

Bats looped over and under the telephone wires. In an all-night diner a waitress served hamburgers to a young couple holding hands.

At the rear of the train stood a man with a lantern. Every now and then he would sing out, "All's well!"

The train went so fast it seemed to fly. At the top of the tallest city building a small red light blinked off and on. Inside the building, workers polished the doorknobs and swept the floors. A late-night disc jockey played a love song dedicated to Laura. And Laura heard it. The grass grew on front lawns. A white moth hovered near a street lamp. People stayed up late and watched TV.

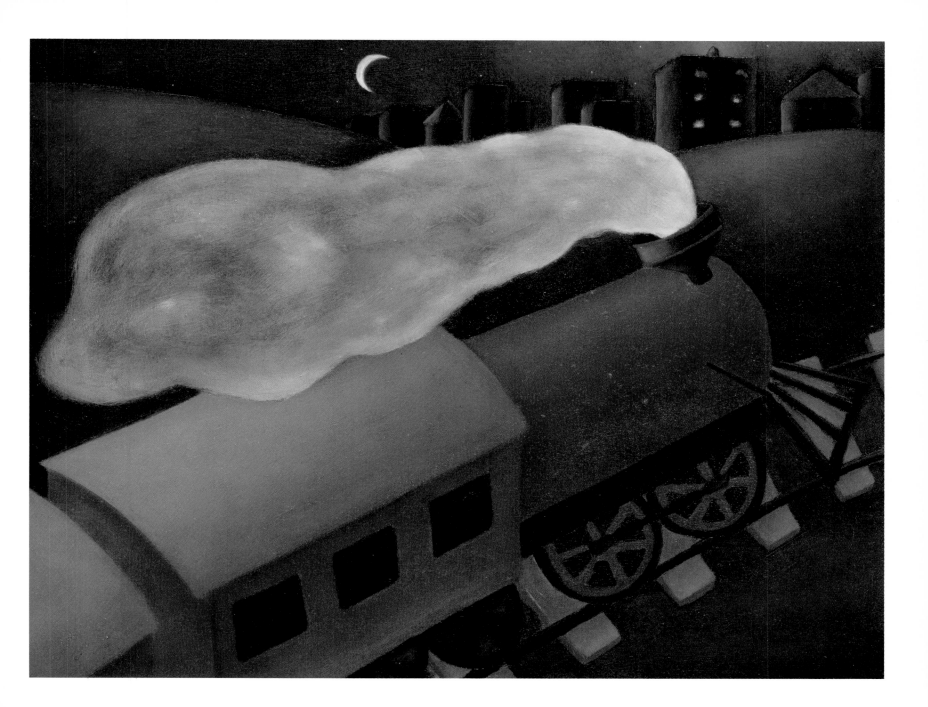

The train slowed and went into a tunnel. It came out again, blew its horn like a harmonica, and came to a whistling stop.

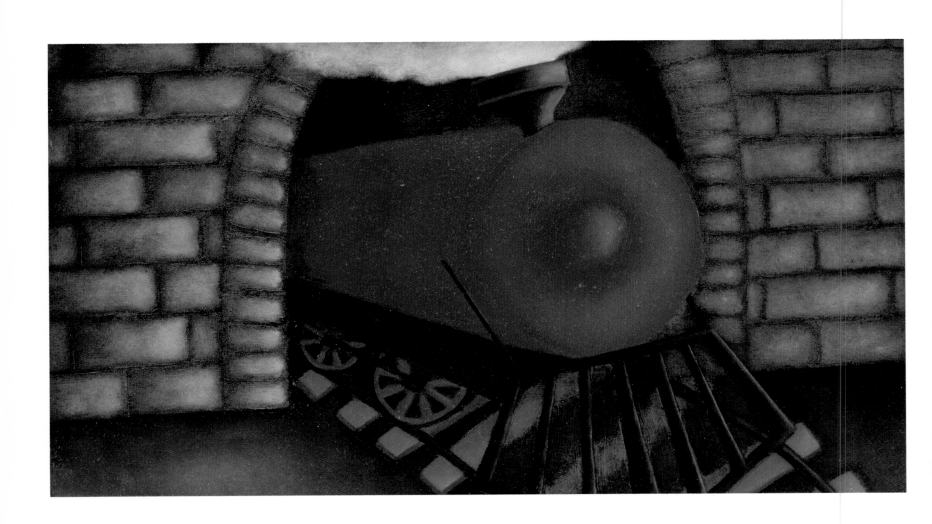

"We're here," the conductor said. He helped Adelaide off the train and onto the empty platform. The air was warm and still, and the sky full of winking stars.

Everything was asleep. There were flowers with their petals folded up like umbrellas for the night. Birds slept huddled together in the trees. Adelaide walked

carefully among the sleeping things. The man who
stood at the back of the train dimmed his lamp and
walked at Adelaide's side. "All's well," he whispered.

The wind rested in the branches of the trees. Horses slept standing up. Babies napped in their cribs, and grown-ups in their beds, and one woman dozed in a hammock between two oaks. A milkman dreamed he was an astronaut, and an astronaut dreamed he was delivering the milk. Even the sun slept behind a hill. It was peaceful there, and Adelaide wished she could stay.

But the conductor cried, "Board!"

So the train hurried back the way it had come, past the houses with their windows shining, past the wakeful city, past the all-night diner. Deer stepped carefully down the hillside, watching the train pass. Clouds raced overhead, playing tag with the moon. A sleepy policewoman walked up and down the street. And a baker slid fresh loaves of bread out of the oven.

"All's well!" cried the man with the lantern.

They passed the blinking lighthouse and the ocean, and the field near Adelaide's house where rabbits still leaped under the moonlight.

At last the train came to a stop, and the conductor let down the metal stairs again and held Adelaide's hand as she stepped into her room. He tucked the covers around her and said, "Good night."

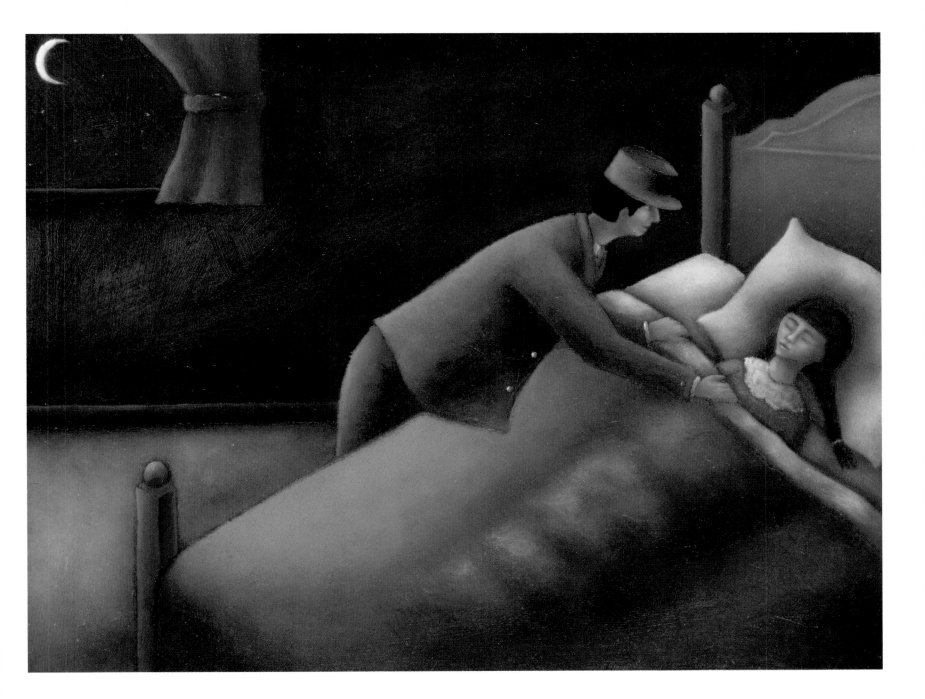

On nights when Adelaide couldn't sleep, she listened for the train. As soon as it passed by, she began to feel sleepy, for she knew where it was going. Often the last thing she heard before she fell asleep was the distant voice of the man with the lantern, calling, "All's well."